DATE DUE

MAR 1 6 2004		
MAY 1 2 2004	FEB 1 6 2012	
MAY 0 3 2005	MAR 1 6 2015	
AUG 2 3 2005	FEB 1 8 2016	
OCT 0 3 2006	MAY 2 6 2016	
APR 2 1	MAR 0 6 2017	
APR 2 4 2008		
AUG 1 8 2009		

Anne S. Bittker
Children's Collection

NEW HAVEN
FREE PUBLIC
LIBRARY

Dr. Friedman Helps Animals

written by
ALICE K. FLANAGAN

photographs by
CHRISTINE OSINSKI

Reading Consultant
LINDA CORNWELL
Learning Resource Consultant
Indiana Department of Education

CHILDREN'S PRESS® *A Division of Grolier Publishing*
New York • London • Hong Kong • Sydney • Danbury, Connecticut

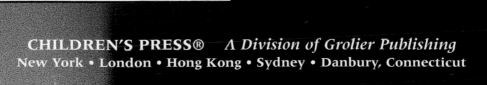

*Dr. Friedman dedicates this book to Vic,
for making everything perfectly clear.*

*Special thanks to Ellen Friedman
for allowing us to tell her story.*

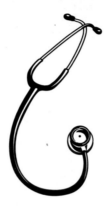

Visit Children's Press® on the Internet at:
http://publishing.grolier.com

Library of Congress Cataloging-in-Publication Data

Flanagan, Alice K.
   Dr. Friedman helps animals / written by Alice K. Flanagan ; photographs by Christine Osinski ; reading consultant, Linda Cornwell.
      p.   cm. – (Our neighborhood)
   Summary: Introduces the work of a veterinarian.
   ISBN 0-516-21138-2 (lib.bdg.)   0-516-26538-5 (pbk.)
   1. Veterinary medicine—Juvenile literature. 2. Veterinarians—Juvenile literature. 3. Veterinary hospitals—Juvenile literature. [1. Veterinarians. 2. Occupations.] I. Osinski, Christine, ill. II. Title. III. Series: Our neighborhood (New York, N.Y.)
SF756.F53 1999
636.089—dc21   98-46562
                                                                              CIP
                                                                              AC

Photographs ©: Christine Osinski

GROLIER
PUBLISHING

© 1999 by Alice K. Flanagan and Christine Osinski
All rights reserved. Published simultaneously in Canada
Printed in the United States of America
1 2 3 4 5 6 7 8 9 10 R 08 07 06 05 04 03 02 01 00 99

Look! There's a lost dog. He might be hurt.

3

Someone calls Dr. Friedman. She's an
animal doctor, or a veterinarian.

She hurries over to see the dog
and care for him.

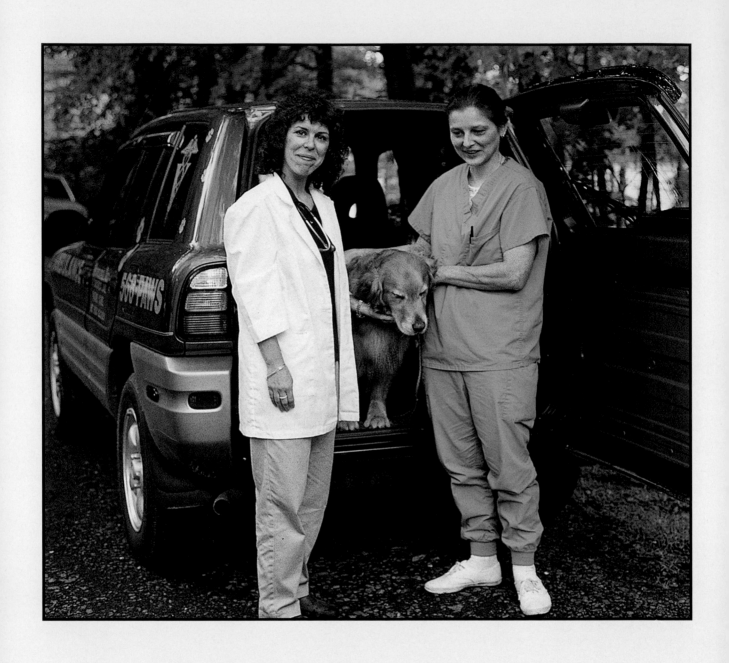

Dr. Friedman takes the dog to the animal hospital so she can examine, or look at him, closely.

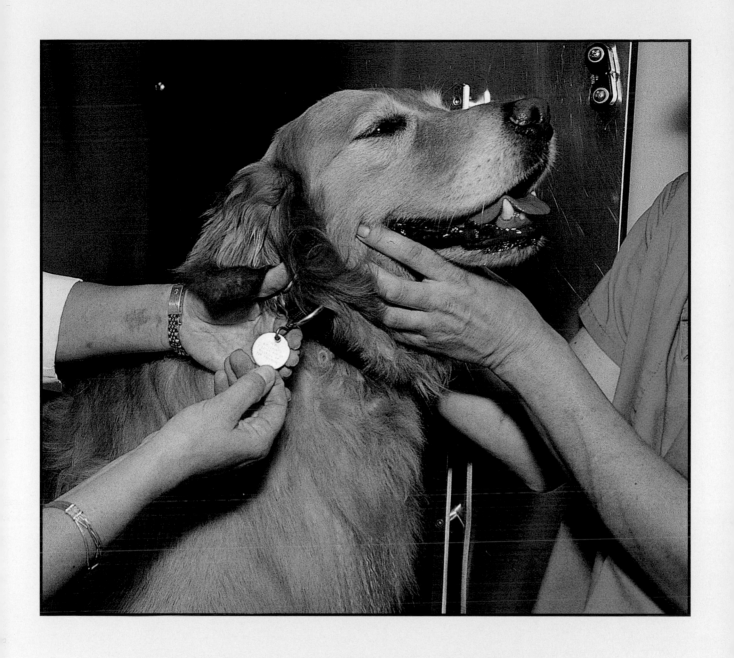

She reads the tag around his neck.
"Your name is Malibu," she says.
"I think you've been here before."

Dr. Friedman looks in her records.
She finds Malibu's name and calls
Malibu's owner.

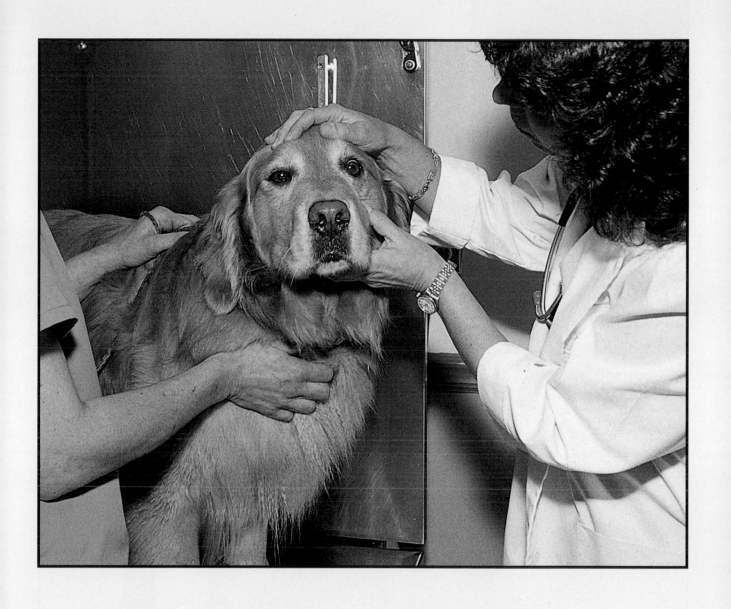

Then she examines Malibu.
She looks in his eyes and ears.
She listens to his heart.

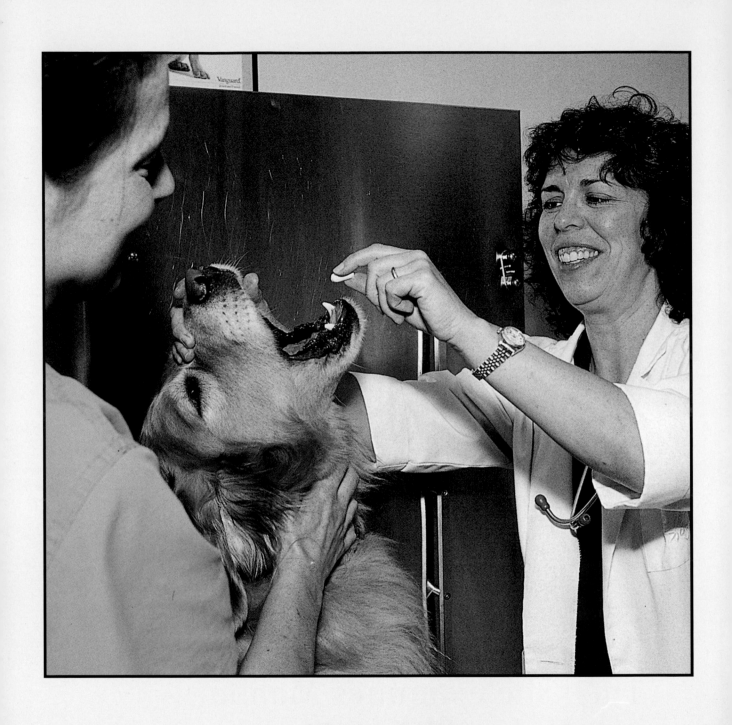

She gives Malibu a pill

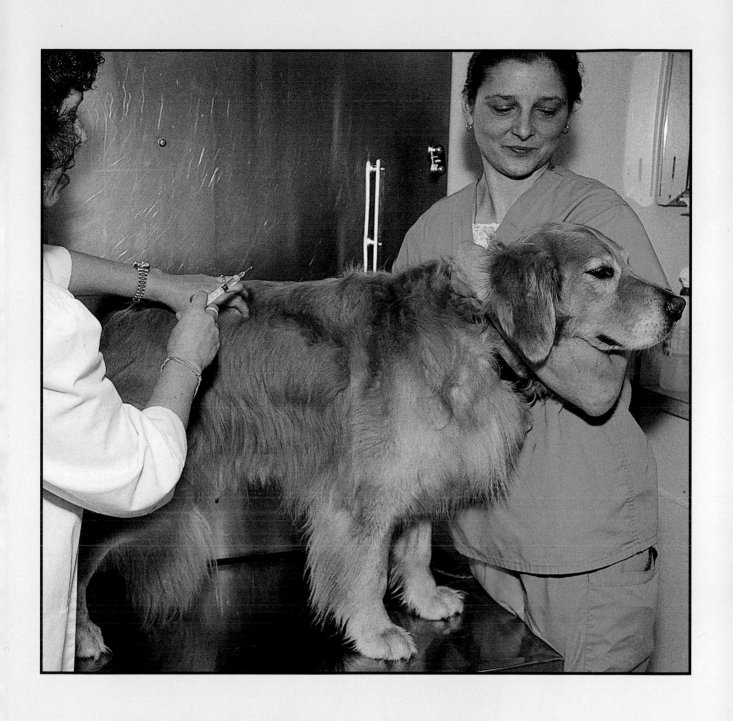

and also a shot.

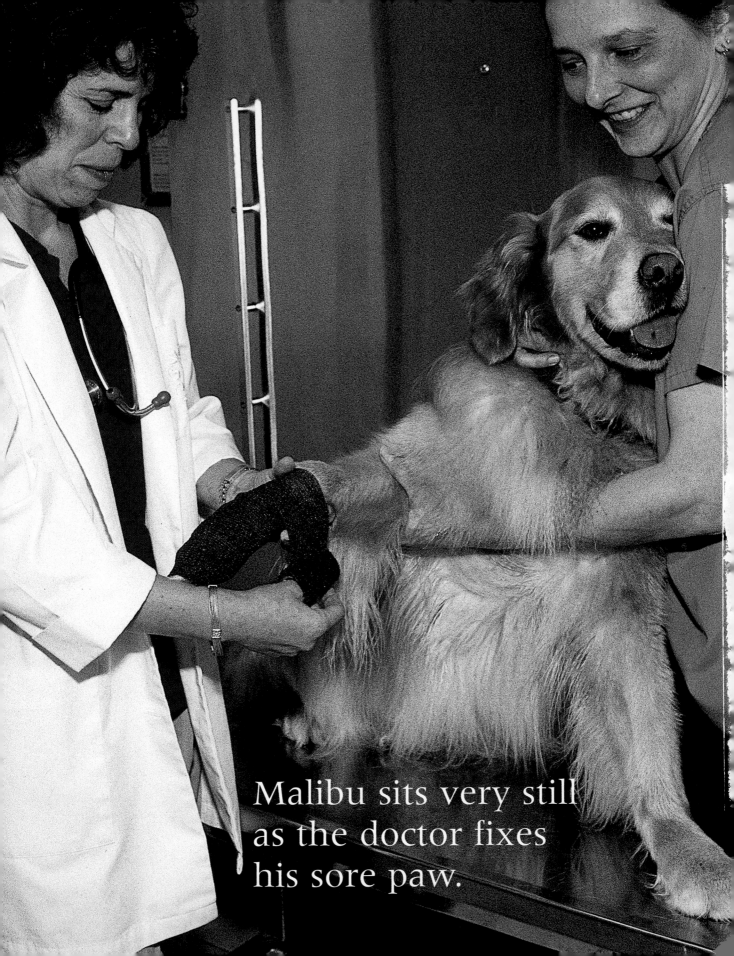

Malibu sits very still
as the doctor fixes
his sore paw.

Finally, Malibu is ready to go home.
Dr. Friedman says good-bye to him
and good luck.

Then, Dr. Friedman begins her
hospital rounds. She checks the
animals that stayed in the hospital
overnight. Some of them are boarders.

They stay at the hospital while their owners are out of town. The wild animals stay at the hospital until they are well.

Dr. Friedman's staff makes sure
the boarders are bathed, brushed,
and fed.

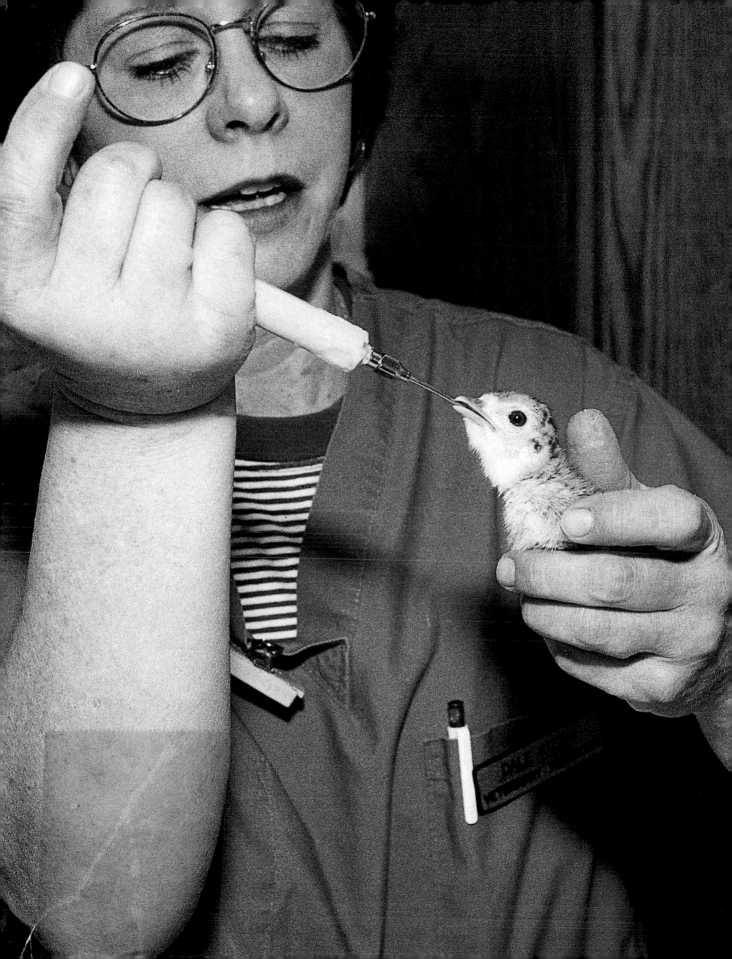

Then Dr. Friedman visits her patients. This is Molly. She is in the hospital because she won't eat.

And here is a little bird that was hit by a car. It might have a broken wing.

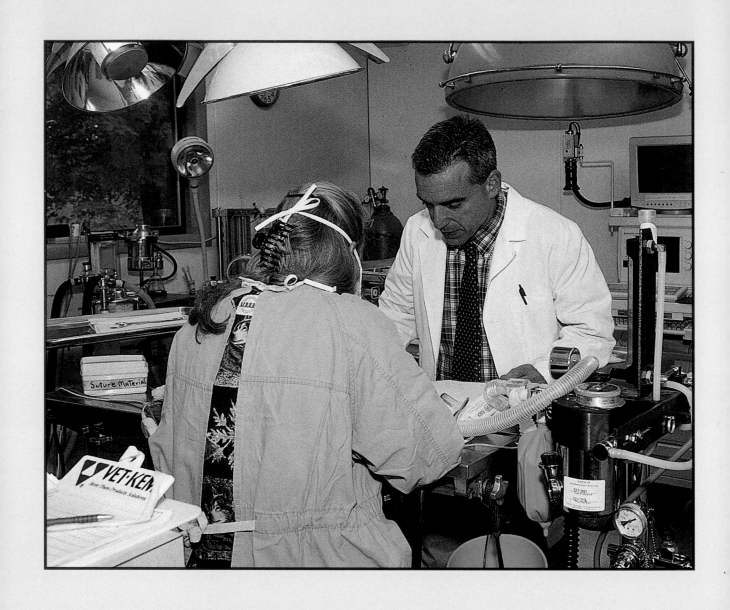

Dr. Friedman's husband works
with her at the hospital. Other
veterinarians work with her, too.

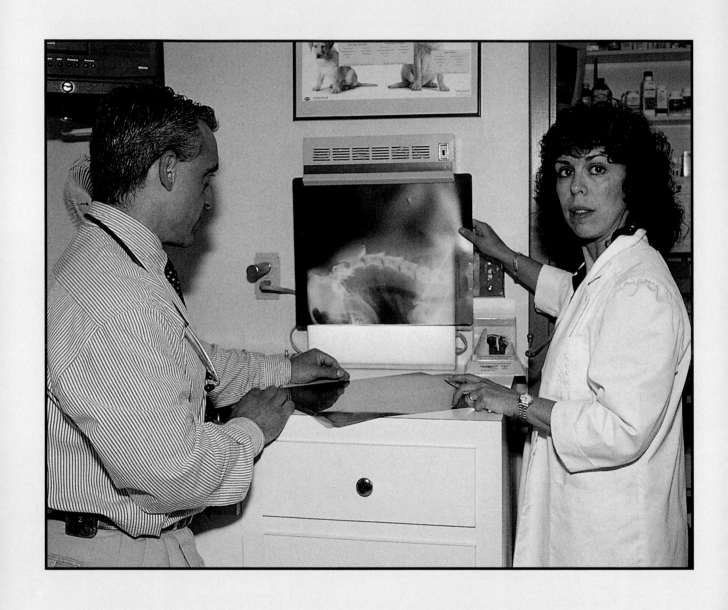

On some days of the week, Dr. Friedman looks at X rays and operates on animals.

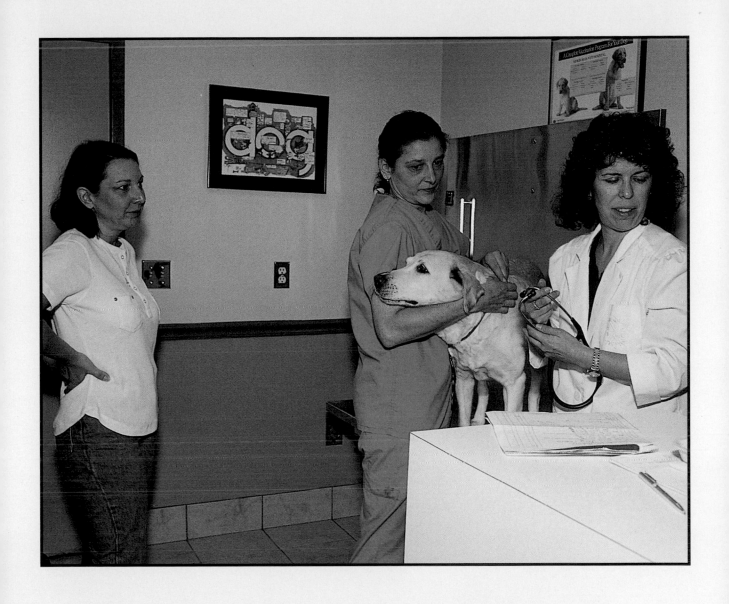

On other days, she examines the
animals that are brought in for
checkups.

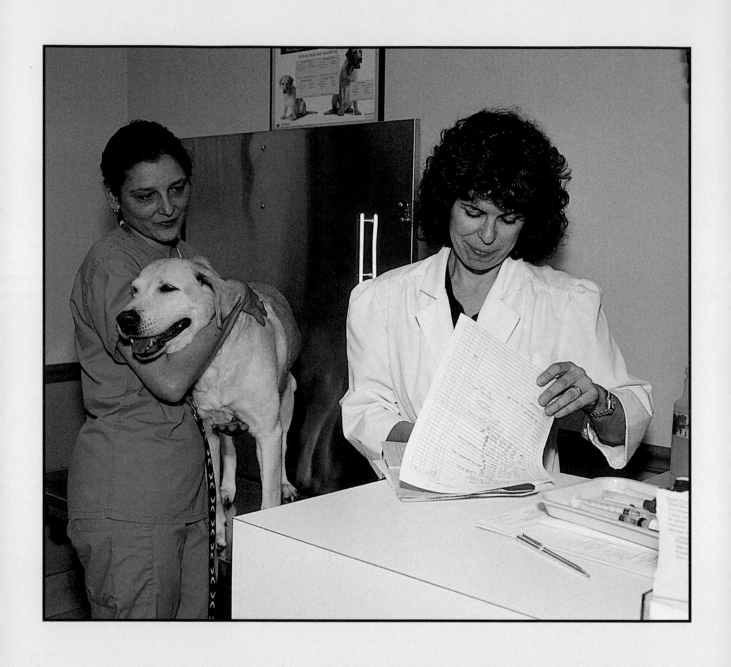

Dr. Friedman keeps careful records
of all her patients.

She writes down
the names of the
medicines she
gives them.

Dr. Friedman studied hard to become a veterinarian. After graduating from high school, she went to school for nine more years. Now Dr. Friedman sometimes works fifteen hours a day.

Dr. Friedman loves being around animals. She says, "I like helping animals and healing them when they're hurt."

Pet owners are grateful to Dr. Friedman for keeping their pets healthy.

The pets have their own special way of saying, "Thanks, Dr. Friedman, you're the best!"

Meet the Author
and the Photographer

Alice Flanagan and Christine Osinski are sisters. They grew up together telling stories and drawing pictures in a brown brick bungalow in a southwest-side neighborhood of Chicago, Illinois. Today they write stories and take photographs professionally.

Ms. Flanagan resides in Chicago with her husband and works as a freelance writer. Ms. Osinski is a photographer and teaches at The Cooper Union for the Advancement of Science and Art in New York City. She lives with her husband and two sons in Ridgefield, Connecticut.